Find Scruncheon and Touton 2

all around Newfoundland

Canada Council Conseil des Arts
for the Arts du Canada

Canada

 Newfoundland
Labrador

We gratefully acknowledge the financial support of the Canada Council for the Arts, the Government of Canada through the Canada Book Fund (CBF), and the Government of Newfoundland and Labrador through the Department of Tourism, Culture and Recreation for our publishing program.

Published by
TUCKAMORE BOOKS
an imprint of CREATIVE BOOK PUBLISHING
a Transcontinental Inc. associated company
P.O. Box 8660, St. John's,
Newfoundland and Labrador
A1B 3T7

Printed in Canada by:
Transcontinental Inc.

Printed on acid-free paper

Library and Archives Canada Cataloguing in Publication

Keating, Nancy
    Find Scruncheon and Touton 2 : all around Newfoundland / Nancy Keating and Laurel Keating.

ISBN 978-1-897174-89-0

    1. Newfoundland and Labrador–Juvenile literature. 2. Dogs– Juvenile literature.
3. Picture puzzles–Juvenile literature. I. Keating, Laurel, 1990- II. Title.

FC2161.2.K43 2012   j971.8   C2012-901097-9

Find Scruncheon and Touton 2
all around Newfoundland

Nancy Keating & Laurel Keating

Tuckamore Books
a Creative Publishers imprint

St. John's, Newfoundland and Labrador
2012

Say 'hi' to Scruncheon;
a big, friendly
Newfoundland Dog...

...and his friend, Touton;
she's a playful
Labrador Retriever!

They're hiding in the familiar Newfoundland and Labrador scenes throughout
the book. See if you can find them, along with the other hidden objects.

At the Bird Sanctuary, find Scruncheon and...

message in a bottle

wishbone

trashcan

fork

anchor

camera

3 boats

lost hat

whistle

axe

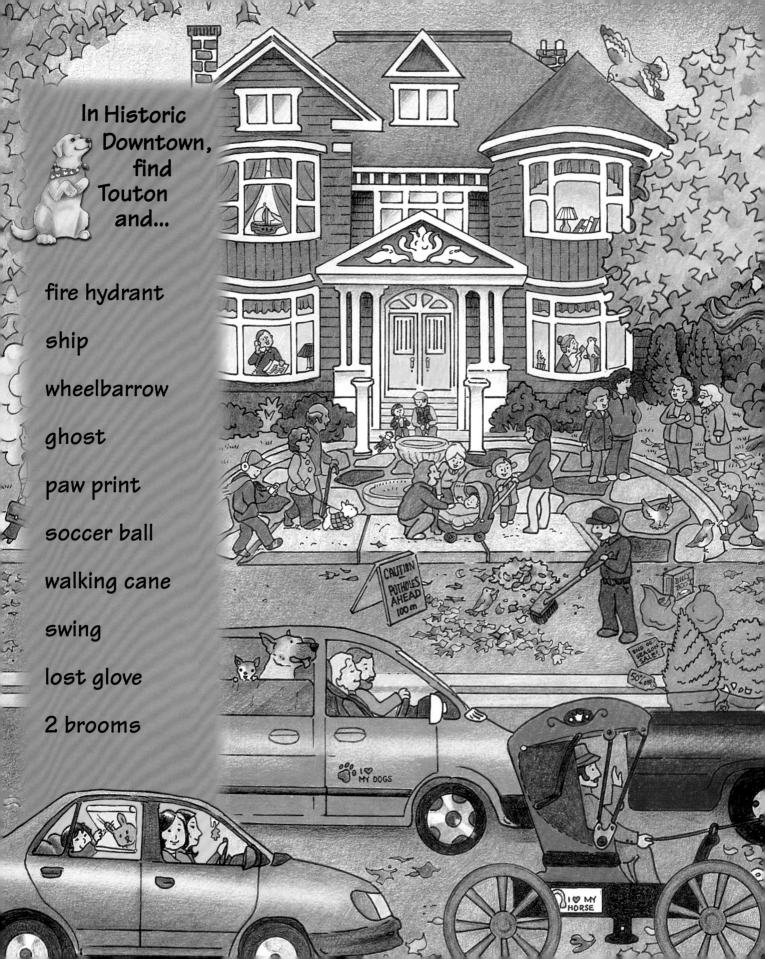

In Historic Downtown, find Touton and...

- fire hydrant
- ship
- wheelbarrow
- ghost
- paw print
- soccer ball
- walking cane
- swing
- lost glove
- 2 brooms

At the Flea Market, find Scruncheon and...

fish tank

toy panda

snowman

umbrella

earmuffs

saxophone

globe

magic wand

watering can

drill

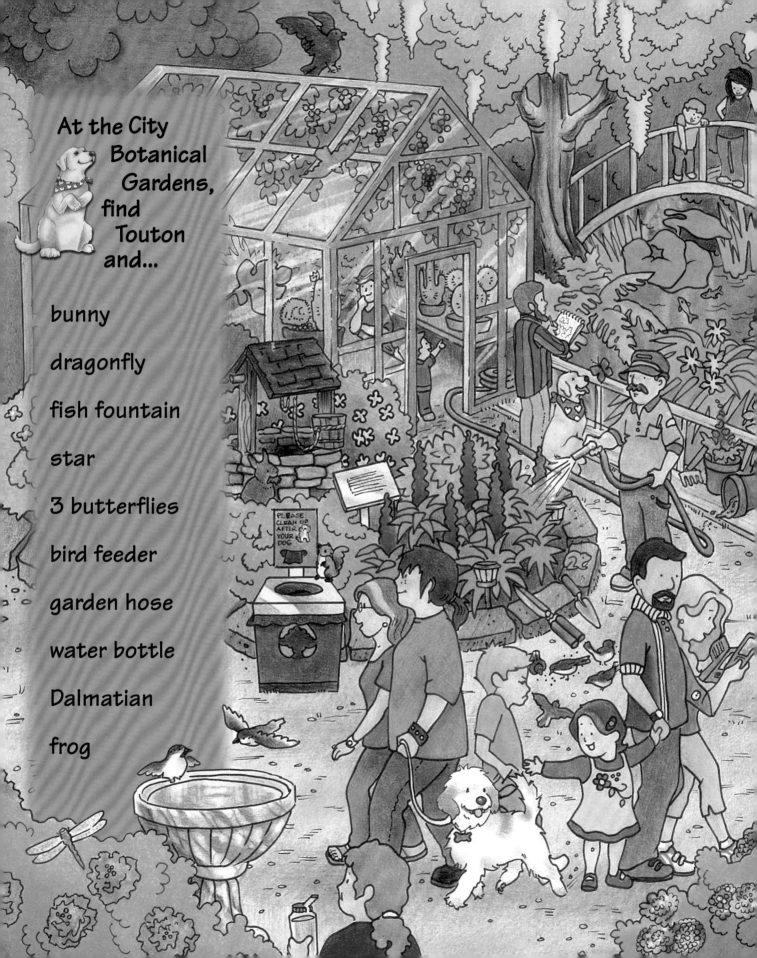

At the City Botanical Gardens, find Touton and...

bunny

dragonfly

fish fountain

star

3 butterflies

bird feeder

garden hose

water bottle

Dalmatian

frog

At the Waterfront, find Scruncheon and...

toy puffin

hotdog

cowboy hat

toy bunny

paw print

2 hearts

guitar

starfish

high chair

maple leaf

At the Kite Festival, find Touton and...

pencil

3 squirrels

toy truck

recycling bin

bunch of bananas

thermos

football

key

twin babies

2 books

In Nanny's Attic, find Scruncheon and...

toy elephant

walking cane

baseball glove

pair of skates

typewriter

candle

magnifying glass

plate of cookies

toy train

bird cage

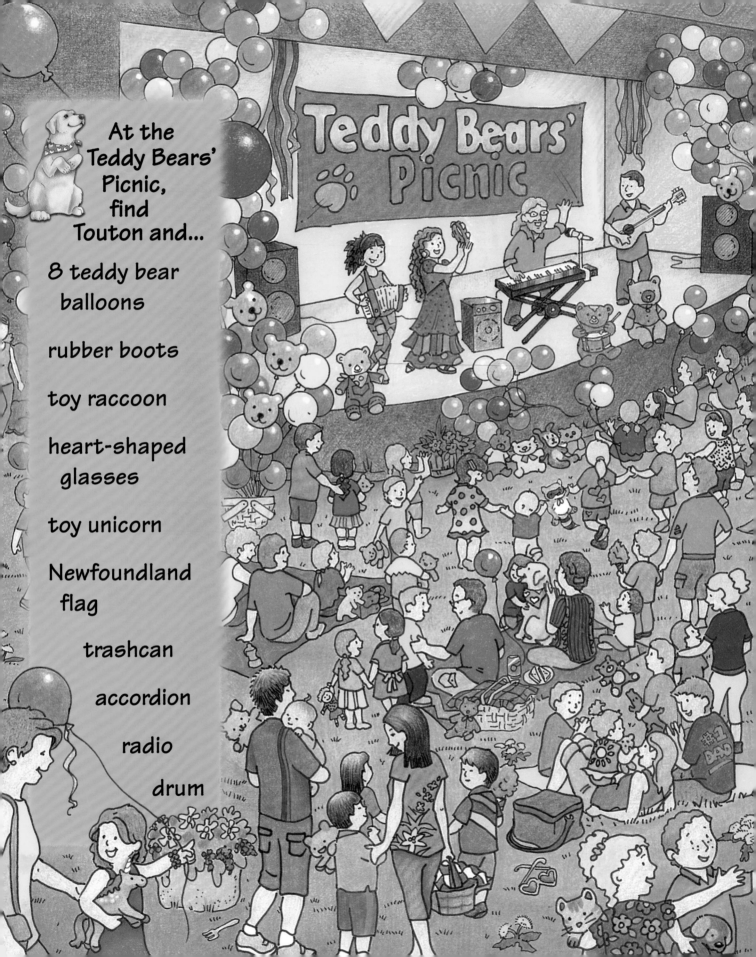

At the
Teddy Bears'
Picnic,
find
Touton and...

8 teddy bear
balloons

rubber boots

toy raccoon

heart-shaped
glasses

toy unicorn

Newfoundland
flag

trashcan

accordion

radio

drum

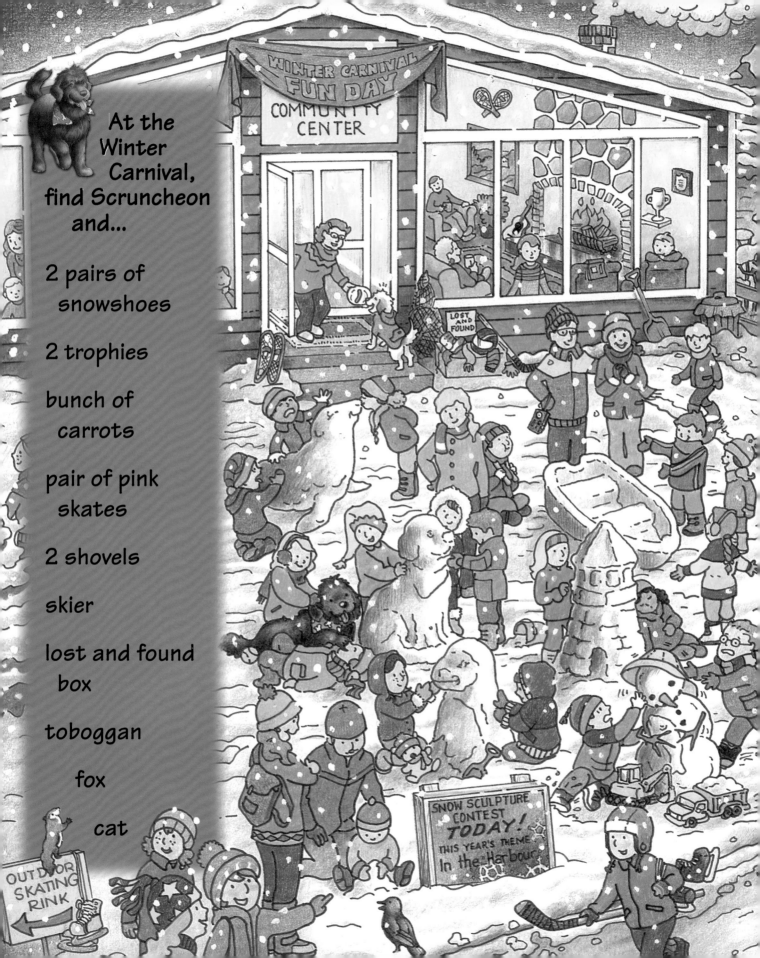

At the Winter Carnival, find Scruncheon and...

2 pairs of snowshoes

2 trophies

bunch of carrots

pair of pink skates

2 shovels

skier

lost and found box

toboggan

fox

cat

At the Capelin Roll, find Touton and...

- teddy bear
- toy boat
- lizard
- flashlight
- guitar
- starfish
- pair of socks
- inflatable swimming ring
- binoculars
- shovel

PLEASE DO NOT LEAVE FIRES UNATTENDED
Thank You!

JAM JAMS

At the Fishing Museum, find Scruncheon and...

crown

2 cats

butterfly

horseshoe

ice cream cone

eagle

feather

crab

rubber boot

2 stuffed toy whales

Now go back through the book again
and see if you can find these pictures, too...

... and these!